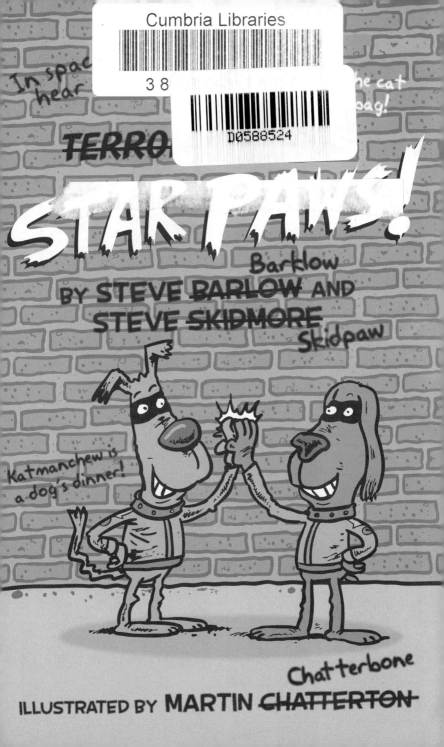

In space... hear... ...the cat ...bag!

~~TERROR~~

# STAR PAWS!

BY STEVE ~~BARLOW~~ **Barklow** AND
STEVE ~~SKIDMORE~~ **Skidpaw**

Katmanchew is a dog's dinner!

ILLUSTRATED BY **MARTIN ~~CHATTERTON~~** **Chatterbone**

# WHO ARE THE ACTION DOGS?

FOR THOUSANDS OF YEARS, DOGS HAVE
BEEN MAN'S BEST FRIEND.

THEY HAVE LOOKED
AFTER OUR ANIMALS AND
GUARDED OUR HOMES.

THEY HAVE HELPED US
HUNT FOR OUR FOOD.

THEY HAVE HELPED
POLICE TO TRACK
DOWN CRIMINALS.

THEY HAVE RESCUED
PEOPLE LOST IN THE
SNOW, OR BURIED BY
EARTHQUAKES.

BUT IN THE TWENTY-FIRST CENTURY, THE WORLD HAS BECOME MUCH MORE COMPLICATED.

OUR HOMES ARE GUARDED BY BURGLAR ALARMS AND CCTV.

WE BUY FOOD FROM THE SUPERMARKET INSTEAD OF CHASING IT.

WE HAVE SPECIAL HEAT-SEEKING CAMERAS TO FIND MISSING PEOPLE.

HUMAN BEINGS HAVE BECOME A LOT CLEVERER.

...deep under the pound is something far from ordinary: the secret headquarters of the famous

HEROIC HOUNDS WHOSE PAW-POSE IN LIFE IS TO SAVE HUMANS IN DISTRESS

And the Action Station, home to their fabulous machines.

THE FLYING FRISBEE
CATCH IT IF YOU CAN!

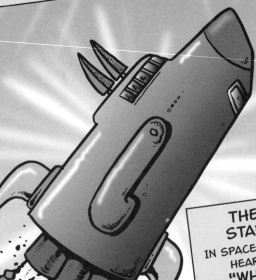

THE DOG STARSHIP
IN SPACE NO ONE CAN HEAR YOU GO "WHEEEE!"

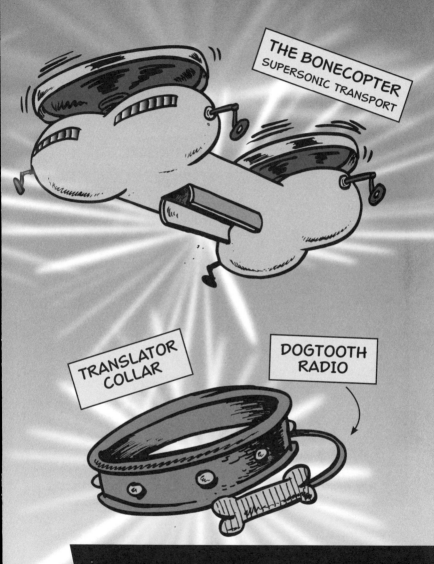

THE BONECOPTER
SUPERSONIC TRANSPORT

TRANSLATOR
COLLAR

DOGTOOTH
RADIO

Our heroes work like dogs to perform their daring rescues and save humans from disaster. But they don't always lead a dog's life – just at the moment they are relaxing between missions ...

Yapper raised his voice in an excited yelp. "Come on, Sally, it's starting!"

Sally rushed to join him on the sofa.

Yapper pressed a button on the remote control.

"*You join us today,*" burbled the TV announcer, "*at the Mohairy Desert Spaceport. Here, beneath the scorching midday sun, excited passengers are about to join Richard Boneson on his latest Maiden Galactic spaceship."*

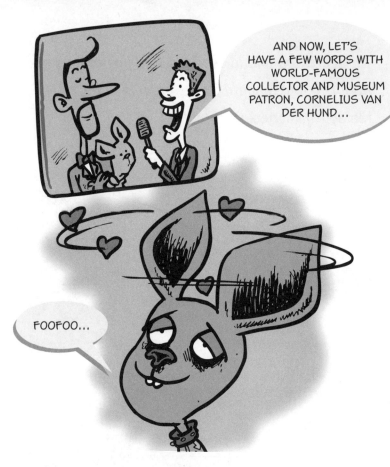

Sally looked from the TV to Yapper and back again. "Oho!"

Yapper tried to look innocent. "Oho, what?"

"You've fancied Foofoo for ages," chortled Sally, "she's your pin-up pooch!"

"No she isn't!" said Yapper.

"So why do you watch TV whenever Mr. Van Der

Hund is on? Because you know he'll have Foofoo with him, that's why! You knew he'd take her to the *Earthview* with him. So you asked Janet to sit in at the Listening Post in case a mission came in while you were watching the spaceship take off for the *Earthview*."

"Well, so what if I do like Foofoo?" said Yapper crossly.

"Poor Yapper. I'm only teasing," Sally told him. "I'm glad you're watching the programme with me."

Sally and Yapper nearly went flying as the other Action Dogs piled in.

"Oops! Sorry, Sally," Benji giggled.

Sally pointed. "What on earth is that thing?"

"It's my latest invention!" said Murdoch proudly. "I call it the Doggy Basket. And it isn't anything on earth. Once it's been tested, we can use it to go outside the Dog Starship without having to put on a spacesuit."

"Well, if it's meant to fly in space," said Sally crossly, "don't fly it around in the Action Station. It's dangerous."

"Nonsense!" snapped Murdoch.

Spike climbed out of the Doggy Basket. Murdoch gazed at it and rubbed his chin. "I'm thinking maybe the controls need a little more work..."

Sally took a mirror from her pocket and checked her furstyle. She gave Spike a disgusted look. "Boys!" she snapped. "Why can't you take an interest in anything except your crazy machines?"

"Keep your fur on," growled Spike, dusting himself off. "Anyway, why can't soppy girls think about anything apart from how they look in a mirror?"

"Will you stop arguing?" pleaded Yapper. "We're missing the show!" The others gathered round the sofa to watch the screen as famous passengers arrived to be taken to the brand-new space hotel.

Sally sighed. "I wish I was going, too," she said dreamily. "According to the tourist brochure, the *Earthview* is the last word in luxury. Its guests have ten-star accommodation and views to die for – *and* the sort of suntan you just cannot get down here."

Sally rolled her eyes. "I might have known you wouldn't understand."

"*And now*," gushed the TV announcer, "*the cabin doors are shut...and the spaceship is rolling towards the end of the runway... A few last checks...and... THERE SHE GOES!*"

The intercom chimed. The captain of *Katbird 1* announced, "Mighty lord, please prepare for landing."

Katmanchew, the most evil cat in the world and sworn enemy of the Action Dogs, took a sip of his cream soda. "I suppose you are wondering, faithful Katnip, why I have left my Himalayan stronghold and ordered my private executive jet to fly to this insignificant island."

I ASSUMED MY LORD FELT IN NEED OF A HOLIDAY.

The notorious crime lord gave an evil chuckle. "Not a bit of it. We are not here to lie on a beach – and our business involves a device far more deadly than a bucket and spade."

Without a flicker of expression, Katnip replied, "I quiver with anticipation to learn your dreadful plan."

The *Katbird 1* switched to hover mode and floated down. It settled on a hidden landing pad with the gentlest of bumps.

Katmanchew rose from his seat. "Come with me, Katnip. Oh, and by the way, that clumsy landing almost made me spill my drink..."

As the screams of the luckless pilot sent flocks of squawking mynah birds fleeing from the treetops, Katnip followed his master down the aeroplane steps. They climbed into an electric buggy whose nervous driver set off down an avenue of palm trees, taking great care not to jolt his passengers.

At length, they emerged into a brightly-lit cavern. Cats in white coats or coloured overalls scurried around generators, computer terminals and other equipment.

A platform rose from the middle of the floor. And on the platform...

Katnip shielded his good eye with his paw. "Master, is that a laser cannon?"

Katmanchew gave an evil chuckle. "Exactly, valued slave. We are directly beneath the crater of the extinct volcano of Katkatoa. When the time comes, this laser will rise into its firing position – and then, it begins!"

Katnip gave a polite cough. "Would this be another plan to rule the world, master?"

"And this time," continued the criminal mastermind, his voice rising to a yowl, "my plan is so mind-bogglingly cunning, the detested Action Dogs will be utterly powerless to stop it!"

Mr. Van Der Hund sat down in an armchair and sank back into golden cushions. He leafed through the welcome pack. "Well, I must say, Foofoo," he gushed, "the prices here might be astronomical, but the food sounds absolutely superb. And as for the entertainment – all my favourite musical acts: Mariah Corgi, Britney Spaniels, *Guns N' Rovers*..."

Foofoo yipped excitedly.

"Everyone is here," Mr. Van Der Hund went on. "Politicians, movie stars – look over there, isn't that Arnold Schnauzernegger talking to Brad Pitbull?" He gazed around happily. "I tell you, Foofoo, I'm so glad we came. This is going to be a holiday to remember!"

As scientists and technokats rushed to obey, Katnip spoke up. "Forgive my stupidity, great lord, but I do not see how a laser cannon on a small island in the middle of nowhere is going to help you conquer the world."

"That," growled his master, "is because you have the brains of a flea and the imagination of a rubber mouse."

Katnip bowed low. "It is indeed so, o wise one."

Katmanchew pointed a polished claw at the cannon. "With this weapon, I will destroy the world's communications satellites, one by one."

Katnip nodded. "Your wickedness is truly magnificent, o master. You are indeed the cat's pyjamas. But how will that advance your deplorable scheme?"

"Because, dolt, those satellites carry the internet and most of the world's TV stations: and as they are destroyed, I shall replace them with my own satellites, carrying *my* TV service – KNN!"

The crime lord continued, "Mine will be the only communications satellite network in the whole world. I will control TV, radio and the internet. Knowledge is power, Katnip, and a world in which I control all sources of information is mine for the taking! As a first step, I shall shut down all police communications. My gangs will be able to steal anything at will. I shall launch the greatest crime spree the world has ever seen!"

"An ingenious plan, master."

"Of course it's ingenious, fool! I shall be a greater media moggul than Rupert Murdog!

What's more, my TV station will show only my favourite programmes..."

"But, master, I do not understand why you say the Action Dogs will not be able to stop you..."

Katmanchew gave an evil chuckle. "Because they will never find this island. The laser can only be seen when it rises up into the crater to fire, and its targets will be destroyed before they can report what they have seen."

"And what of the Dog Starship, o great one?"

Katmanchew waved a scornful paw. "The Action Dogs' puny spaceship is no threat to me. And if they do succeed in interfering, my laser cannon will work on a spaceship just as effectively as it will work on a satellite. Observe!"

Katmanchew spoke into a microphone. "Open the crater."

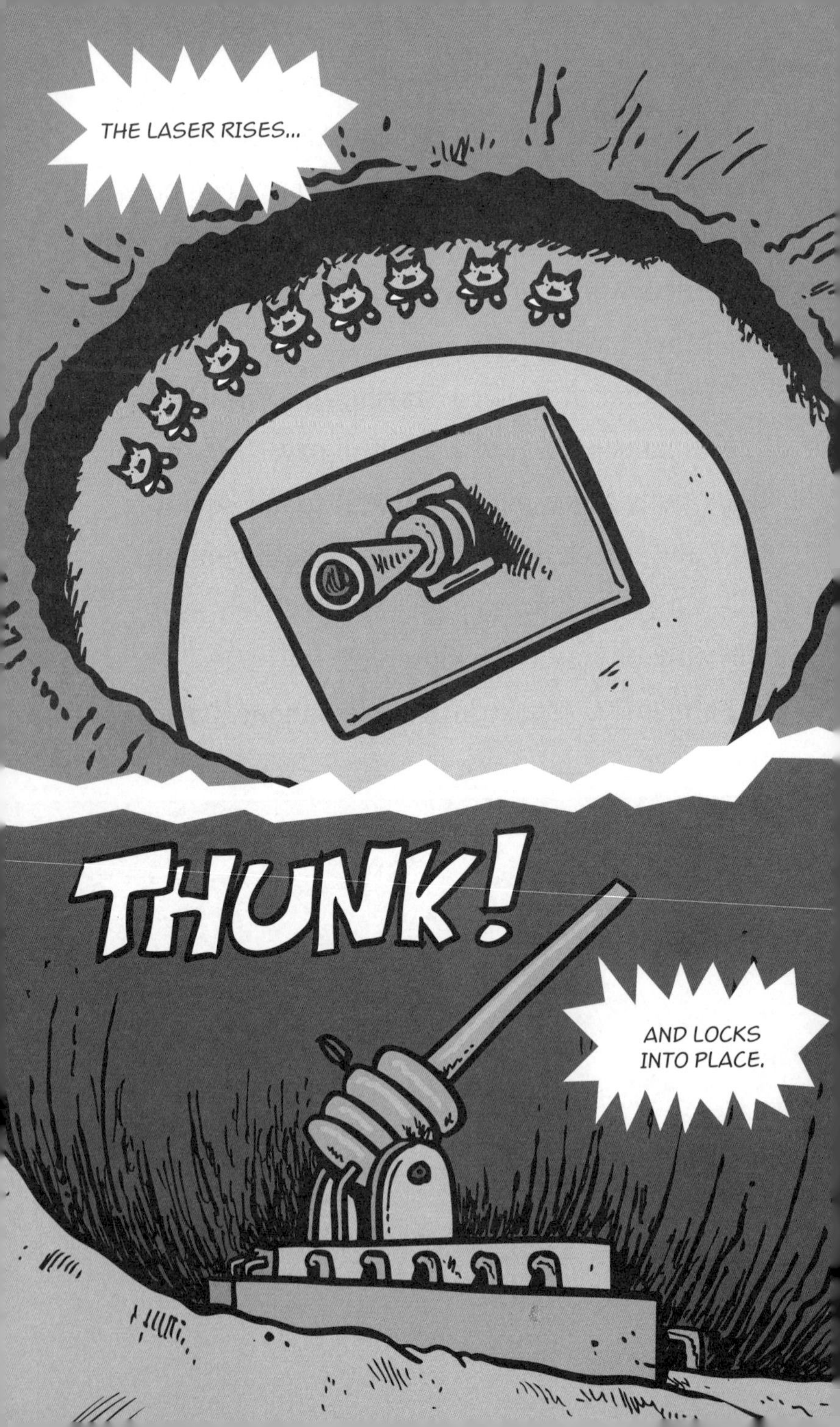
THE LASER RISES...
THUNK!
AND LOCKS INTO PLACE.

Katmanchew pointed to a TV screen. "This shows a live picture from my private space telescope. You see that satellite, Katnip?" His lieutenant nodded. "Very well." The crime lord raised his voice. "Fire!"

"*Hey, team.*" Janet's voice echoed round the Action Station. "*Better get up here.*"

Spike spoke into his dogtooth radio. "Trouble?"

"*I don't know. Could be.*"

"F.I.D.O. – we're on our way."

Spike led the way to the Listening Post, where the Action Dogs monitored world communications for the distress call that might send them on their next mission.

Benji was surprised to see that the team's Taekwondog instructor had already arrived. "Master Yi! I thought you were meditating in the dogjo."

"I was," said the old Pekingese, "but then, I sensed a great disturbance in the universe."

Benji drew in his breath sharply. "You mean, with your astounding and mysterious mental powers, you felt a sudden rift in the very fabric of reality itself?"

"No – watching a Jackie Chan movie on TV, I was, and the picture went."

Spike stared at the screen. "What happened to it? Satellites don't blow up just like that!"

Murdoch shook his head. "Did you no' see that beam of light that hit the satellite just before it exploded? Looked to me as if it came from a laser cannon."

Rascal nodded wisely. "Twinkle, twinkle, little light – blew that baby outta sight!"

"Katmanchew!" snapped Sally. "I'll bet he's behind this."

Spike looked grim. "If Katmanchew has got his paws on a laser cannon, he could do no end of damage."

Yapper had joined Janet at the Listening Post controls. Now he held up a paw for quiet. "I've just picked up something interesting from a United Nations Earth Survey spaceship, the *Argus*. The crew is taking satellite images of the whole planet to update our digital maps."

"Let's see it," ordered Spike.

Yapper's paws flew over the touchscreen controls. "This is the picture being sent by the *Argus*."

The Action Dogs listened carefully as the call
continued:

"*This is mission control – go ahead* Argus. *Over.*"

"*Mission control, we just spotted a bright flash of
light somewhere in the Java Sea. Do you have any
reports of weapons firing in that area, over?*"

"Argus, *that's a negative, we have no reports of
firing at this time, over.*"

"Copy that. Our orbit is taking us away from that location: when we overfly again in ninety minutes, we'll take a close look at where we saw the flash and try to identify the source. Over."

Yapper turned the sound down. "What do we do?"

"Keep watching and listening," said Spike. "The satellite might still have blown up by accident."

"I doubt it," said Murdoch. "On the other paw, why would Katmanchew blow up a communications satellite?"

NO IDEA, BUT IF KATMANCHEW REALLY IS BEHIND THIS, HE'S BOUND TO SHOW HIMSELF – SOONER OR LATER.

INCOMPETENT BUFFOON! YOU SWORE TO ME THAT YOU COULD KEEP THIS ISLAND HIDDEN FROM MY ENEMIES!

Katmanchew's chief scientist cowered. "Mercy, mighty lord! We did not know about the Earth Survey ship *Argus*..."

"But now, they know about us, numbskull! Did you not hear their message?"

"But they do not know exactly where we are – there are many islands, and the laser cannon is hidden..."

"Silence, fool!" spat Katmanchew. He gestured to Katnip. "I don't suppose the sharks found my pilot much more than a starter. The poor things must still be hungry – they can have this idiot for their main course."

At Katnip's signal, two burly hench-cats closed in to drag the shrieking scientist away.

Katmanchew's eyes narrowed in thought. "In ninety minutes, the orbit of the Earth Survey ship will bring it overhead again."

DOES THAT MATTER, GREAT LORD, IF THE LASER CANNON IS HIDDEN?

"We cannot take any chances," growled Katmanchew. "The crew may know more than they are saying. In any case, as long as that ship remains in orbit, I cannot use the cannon for fear

that they will find us. No, Katnip, I will not sit here
like a rat in a cellar, waiting for my enemies to hunt
me down. Prepare the laser for firing!"

"Are you sure that is wise, my lord?"

DON'T QUESTION
ME, IMBECILE! THE
MOMENT THAT SHIP'S
ORBIT BRINGS IT
WITHIN RANGE OF MY
LASER, I SHALL BLAST
IT OUT OF THE SKY!

MURDOCH –
HAVE YOU FINISHED
THE FLIGHT CHECKS ON
THE FLYING FRISBEE?

AYE – SHE'S
READY TO GO!

"What's the plan?" asked Benji.

Spike checked the time on the Action Station clock. "The *Argus* will be over the Java Sea again in a few minutes – if they can pinpoint the island where they saw the flash, we'll take the Flying Frisbee and check it out."

"Why the Flying Frisbee? Why not the Bonecopter?"

"The Frisbee is faster – and we don't know whether we'll need any heavy equipment until we find out what caused the flash." Spike checked the time again. "Come on – we'd better get back to the Listening Post and see what's going on."

The Action Dogs listened intently to the radio message between the ship and mission control:

"*Mission control, this is* Argus. *We're over the search area now. Nothing to report.*"

"Argus, *scan the area with your cameras. We can check the footage later."*

"*Copy that, control."*

The picture of the astronauts on the TV monitors was replaced by one from the survey ship's cameras. It showed a wide area of sea, rippled by waves and dotted with islands.

For a while, nothing happened. Then one of the astronauts said, "*Control, this is* Argus. *I just saw something on an island to the south-west... I'll try and zoom in closer..."*

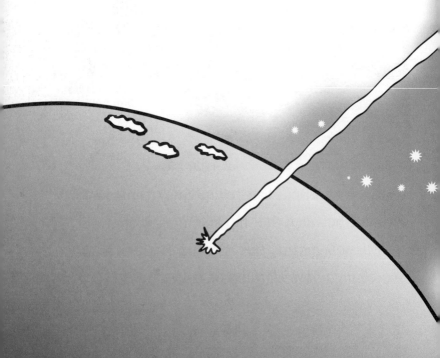

Sally stared at the TV monitor, which now showed only an interference pattern. "What happened?"

Yapper was busy at his controls. "I've lost the radio signal from the *Argus*... Wait, they're transmitting again on an emergency frequency!"

A few moments later, a faint voice came over the radio:

MAYDAY, MAYDAY. ALL STATIONS, THIS IS UN EARTH SURVEY SHIP ARGUS. THE VESSEL IS BADLY DAMAGED. WE HAVE LOST ENGINES AND MAIN COMMUNICATIONS – WE ARE DRIFTING OUT OF CONTROL. MAYDAY, MAYDAY...

Spike squared his shoulders. "Well, that settles it. We're a search and rescue team – and it looks like the search will have to wait. We have a rescue on our paws. This is a job for the Dog Starship!"

SPIKE TO MURDOCH
– WILL YOU HURRY
IT UP?

FIRST YE WANT
THE FLYING FRISBEE, NOW YE
WANT THE DOG STARSHIP – I
WISH YE'D MAKE YOUR MIND UP.
I'VE TOLD YE A MILLION TIMES, I'M
A MECHANIC, NO' A MIRACLE
WORKER!

In the Listening Post, Spike ground his teeth.

"We're wasting time."

"Calm down, Spike," said Sally. "I'm sure Murdoch's doing his best. It takes time to prepare the Dog Starship."

"We don't *have* time," Spike pointed out. "Those guys are in trouble up there..."

He was interrupted by a howl of dismay from Yapper. "No!" groaned the Chihuahua. "No, noooooo..."

"So?" said Spike. "Work out its new course."

"I have," moaned Yapper. "I ran a computer simulation. I'll put it on the big screen."

"That settles it," said Spike grimly. "Whether Murdoch is ready or not, we have to get going!"

"I'm sorry, team," said a new voice, "but you're not going anywhere."

The Action Dogs turned to see Janet standing in the doorway with a shocked expression on her face.

"What are you talking about?" demanded Spike. "We have a mission!"

"Yes, and I've just finished a phone call with Welfare Officer Brick. He's on his way over here now, for a full inspection. And until he goes," said Janet unhappily, "none of us is leaving the pound!"

"I thought, o infamous one, your weapon was supposed to destroy the survey ship," observed Katnip. "Instead it has only damaged it. In what way is this 'excellent'?"

"Because, dolt, many lives are now in danger. Faced with a disaster of kataclysmic proportions, the despicable Action Dogs will launch their Dog Starship to rescue the crew of the survey ship, *and* the guests from the hotel. They will have their paws full. And when they are all busy with their do-gooding, we will be ready for them."

ONCE THE ACTION DOGS ARE OUT OF THE PICTURE, THERE WILL BE NO ONE TO OPPOSE MY MASTER PLAN. THE WORLD WILL BE MINE!

"We have a mission to save hundreds of lives," Spike went on, "and you're saying we have to sit in the pound like a bunch of dumb mutts just because Brick says so? Tell him to get lost!"

"You know I can't do that," said Janet wearily. "Protecting our secret identity is our top priority. Brick won't postpone the inspection, and if you're all missing when he arrives, he'll find out what really goes on around here."

Yapper was horrified. "But what about Foofoo?"

"And the hundreds of humans on *Earthview*," Sally reminded him sharply, "not to mention the crew of the survey ship."

OH YEAH – THEM TOO.

"All right," said Benji. "If we can't stop him coming here, and we have to be up in the pound when he does, all we can do is make sure he goes away again really quickly."

"That makes sense," said Sally. "Can anyone think of a way we can make that happen?"

Master Yi stood up and bowed to the rest of the team...

WHY YES –
I BELIEVE AN IDEA,
I HAVE...

"Oh, I'm sorry, sir," said Janet sympathetically. "I couldn't help noticing you seemed a bit off-colour. Run down."

"Rubbish!" Brick looked a bit less sure of himself. "How do you mean?"

"Well, you know, sir – no spring in your step, bags under your eyes – I just wondered if you were working too hard..."

"Hah!" cried Brick. "Don't talk to me about overwork! They take me for granted at the office, you know."

"I can tell," said Janet. "You look exhausted."

DO I?

OH, I'M SURE IT'S NOTHING, REALLY. TEA?

Janet switched on the kettle, then clicked her tongue. "I forgot the milk. Won't be a moment." She went out, closing the door behind her.

Officer Brick got up and looked in the mirror on Janet's wall.

SHE'S RIGHT – BLOODSHOT EYES, FURRY TONGUE – I DO LOOK A BIT PEAKY...

Just then, the door opened, and a Scottish terrier came in. Normally this wouldn't have been surprising in a dog pound – but this one was wearing a kilt and playing the bagpipes.

Brick watched with his mouth wide open as the dog marched around the office and out again. A moment later, Janet came in carrying a bottle of milk.

Brick pointed at the door. "There was a dog in here, playing the bagpipes!"

"Bagpipes?" Janet looked concerned. "Are you sure you're all right, sir? I'll get your tea – and I think you'd better have some sugar. Very good for shock." She went out again.

A moment later, a Pekingese bounced into the room wearing a full karate suit.

Master Yi twisted and backflipped out through the door and Janet came back in with the sugar. "Why are you hiding under the desk, sir?"

Brick crawled out from his hiding place. His eyes were bulging and his face was the colour of cheese. "There was a P-p-peke doing k-k-karate..."

"Of course there was, sir," said Janet soothingly. "Here's your tea. I'll just get you a nice biscuit."

Brick dropped into his chair as she went out again. Then two dogs came in with a boombox blasting out rap music.

The dogs danced out and Brick dropped back into his chair, gasping for air as Janet came back in with the biscuits.

Brick pointed an accusing finger at her.

Janet sat down at her desk and opened a notebook. "I think you must be seeing things, sir. You're probably having hallucinations brought on by overwork and exhaustion. Do you want to tell me about it? I'll just make some notes." She took a cucumber out of her desk drawer and began to write with it.

Officer Brick groaned. "Yes – hallucinations – that's it. I think I'll just...go to the bathroom and... splash some cold water on my face..."

"Good idea, sir," said Janet brightly.

As soon as Officer Brick had left the room, Janet slipped into the corridor.

Benji reached up to close the hatch – only to
have it snatched from his paws.

Spike looked round angrily. "Yapper – what are you doing here?"

The Chihuahua gave him a defiant glare. "I'm coming, too!"

"No you're not!" barked Spike. "We need you at the Listening Post..."

"Master Yi's at the Listening Post. He's already whipping up a storm."

Benji was confused. "Well, I'm sure he'll do a good job monitoring distress calls, but..."

"No, Benji," said Sally. "Yapper means he really *is* whipping up a storm – a thunderstorm. He's getting one going with Murdoch's climate control system. That's how we can take off in a spaceship without being seen."

Spike was glaring at Yapper.

"We haven't time to argue," said Sally firmly.
"Let him come, Spike."

Spike threw his paws in the air. "All right – just
get strapped in. We've wasted enough time." He
reached for the controls. "Ready?"

"Ready," agreed Sally. "Starting countdown...
thirty seconds...twenty-nine...twenty-eight..."

"We haven't got time for a countdown," roared
Spike. "Zero!" He punched a button labelled
*Engine Start*.

Welfare Officer Brick rushed into Janet's office. He pointed wildly towards the window. "Spaceship!" he gibbered. "Out there! Spaceship – rumbling, flames, whoosh! Ha ha!"

Janet gave him a sympathetic look. "It's all right, sir. It's just the storm."

Brick pointed a quivering finger. "Kennelmaid Janet! Why have you turned into a gorilla????!!!!"

Sally checked her instruments. "That's it – we're in orbit."

"All right," said Spike. "You can take your seat belts off now, team. Murdoch, plot a course so we can catch up with the *Argus*."

"F.I.D.O." Murdoch got busy with the flight computer.

"*Listening Post to Dog Starship.*" Janet's voice sounded tinny and far away. "*Hi, gang. Officer Brick cancelled his inspection. He's gone home for a lie down. The gorilla suit I hired for the fancy dress party last week was the last straw.*"

"Good work, Janet." Spike looked up as Benji floated past his head. "I'll call you later." He switched the radio to standby and glared at Benji. "Will you quit fooling?"

Benji looked sheepish. "Oh yeah – I knew that."

"Right." Spike undid the straps that were holding him into his chair. "We need a plan. We have to stop the *Argus* crashing into the *Earthview* hotel. This is going to be a tough assignment, so I want everyone on the ball, eyes on the prize..."

Benji grabbed hold of a handle to try to stop himself drifting. The handle twisted and a loud electronic voice filled the cabin.

The computer continued the countdown while Murdoch punched at its keyboard. Eventually, the computer announced, "Countdown terminated,"

and Murdoch gave a sigh of relief. "I've stopped the countdown," he said. "I only loaded the Doggy Basket a few hours ago – I don't want it flying off into deep space all by itself before I've even checked that it's working properly!"

"Well done, Murdoch," said Spike. "Benji, don't touch anything else!" He turned to Sally. "Try contacting the *Argus* on the radio."

"F.I.D.O." Sally spoke into her dogtooth radio. "This is Action Dogs vessel Dog Starship calling *Argus*. Come in please, *Argus*. Over."

A moment later a faint voice replied. "*Action Dogs? This is* Argus. *Are we glad to hear you guys!*"

"*Argus*, what is your situation? Over."

"*We've suffered serious damage. We have lost air pressure in the main cabin. We've taken shelter in the airlock: it's the last airtight compartment on the ship. Over.*"

Sally looked worried. "How many of you are there aboard, and are you wearing your spacesuits? Over."

*"There are three of us, and that's a negative – we didn't have time to put them on. Our suits are in the main cabin, and we can't get to them. Over."*

"Stand by." Sally gazed around at the others.

IF THEY CAN'T GET TO THEIR SPACESUITS, HOW CAN WE GET THEM OFF THE ARGUS?

Spike shook his head unhappily. "I don't know. Murdoch, have you worked out that course yet?"

Murdoch didn't look up from his computer screen. "Aye – I've plotted a course that will bring us alongside the *Argus* in fifteen minutes..."

Spike nodded. "Good."

"Aye – but fifteen minutes after *that*, unless we can stop it, the *Argus* will smash into the *Earthview* hotel, killing everyone on board."

THEY'RE ALL DOOMED, I TELL YE! DOOMED!

"Attention, please!" boomed a recorded voice from the hotel loudspeakers. "Our scanners indicate that this hotel is about to be hit by a runaway spaceship. Would all guests please proceed calmly to their emergency stations. We hope this sudden catastrophe does not spoil your holiday pleasure..."

I HEAR THERE'S A SPACESHIP ABOUT TO CRASH INTO US.
THAT IS CORRECT, SIR.

"But this is terrible!" said Mr. Van Der Hund. "What are you doing about it?"

"I'm sure the manager is doing everything possible, sir," said the steward. "In the meantime, I must ask you please to report to your emergency station."

"What for?"

"Because it's your emergency station," said the steward patiently. "It's where you go when there's an emergency."

"You mean, you're sending us back to earth on the ship that brought us here?" said Mr. Van Der Hund hopefully.

"Unfortunately, sir, that ship has already left for earth to pick up more passengers."

"Well then, what about lifeboats?"

"This is a hotel, sir," said the steward. "We don't have lifeboats. We have a small amount of room on one of the catering ships that has just finished delivering food, so the manager has given the order, 'Women and children first', sir."

As the steward made his way between the panicking passengers, Mr. Van Der Hund shook his head. "Well, really! If that's the way they run this hotel, I won't be staying here again – in fact I've half a mind to ask for my money back!"

Katmanchew gave a throaty chuckle. "They must have realized by now that they cannot save both the crew of the *Argus* and the guests in the hotel. They are faced with a terrible choice. It will be amusing to see what they decide to do."

Katnip bowed. "Truly, master, your wickedness knows no bounds."

"Oh, you're just saying that to please me." The fiendish mastermind settled back in his chair. "I shall wait until our flea-ridden friends perform their pointless rescue. If they manage to destroy themselves in the attempt, so much the better. If they succeed – in the very moment of their meaningless triumph, I shall strike! The Action Dogs will be no more, and then nothing will stand in the way of my plan for world domination. Nothing!"

"So what do we do?" asked Benji.

In a low voice, Spike said, "There is one way we could be sure of saving everyone on the *Earthview*. The Dog Starship is carrying missiles for blowing up asteroids that come too close to earth..."

"Listen, Sally," Spike said angrily, "I don't like it either – but if the crew of the *Argus* can't get to their spacesuits, we can't get them out. And while we're wasting time trying, the *Argus* will hit the hotel. Three astronauts on the *Argus*, hundreds of people on the *Earthview*. It's all about numbers."

"I can do the maths as well as you can, Spike," said Sally, "and it doesn't make any difference. Blowing people up is not an option – there has to be another way!"

"Fine!" yelled Spike. "Find another way, and we'll do it!"

"But how could we catch the *Argus*?" demanded Spike.

"Well, we've got manipulator arms for collecting broken satellites, haven't we?" said Benji. "We could catch the *Argus* with those – and we wouldn't have to move it by much, just enough so that it misses the hotel. Once that's safe, we'll have more time to rescue the *Argus*'s crew."

Spike shot a glance at Murdoch. "Would that work?"

"I'm on it." Murdoch punched computer keys for a moment, then looked up.

AYE – WE CAN DO IT.
BUT WE HAV'NAE
MUCH TIME.

"Well done, Benji," said Sally quietly.

Dogs can't blush but Benji did his best.

"All right," said Spike briskly. "Sounds like a plan. Let's get moving, team..."

Spike looked over his shoulder to where Sally was flying the Dog Starship. "Hold your course, Sally."

"Doing my best," said Sally tightly.

"Okay," said Rascal, easing the controls to send the arms forward. "Here we go, that's for sho'... I got it... I got it..."

CREAK!

WHOOPS, DUDES — PARDON ME. GUESS THE ARGUS JUST BROKE FREE. I AIN'T GOT IT.

Sally shook her head. "This is no good. We'll have to start again. I'll try spinning the Dog Starship the same way as the *Argus*. That way, there will be less strain on the grabs."

"Good idea," growled Murdoch, "only there's a problem – we'll need both grabs to steady the *Argus*, and Rascal just broke one."

Spike groaned. "What's wrong with it?"

"It's stuck at half open, and it won't move. I could maybe fix it if I could get inside, but the gap between the jaws is too narrow for me..."

"Not for me," said Yapper. "I'm smaller than you."

Murdoch gave the Chihuahua a calculating look. "Aye, maybe. Ye're a brave laddie for volunteering. There's no way to get to the grab from inside the Dog Starship, so I take it you know what you're letting yourself in for?"

YES, I KNOW – SPACE WALKIES!

The other dogs watched anxiously as Yapper reached the grab. After a few wriggles, he managed to clamber inside.

Murdoch pressed the *transmit* switch on the ship's radio. "Can ye see the problem?"

"*I think so.*" Yapper's voice was quite clear though, because of the helmet, his breathing sounded louder than usual. "*There's a bolt missing – it must have broken off with all the shaking. I'm going to replace it.*"

"F.I.D.O."

After a few moment's grunting and clattering, Yapper said, "*That's it. Try it now.*"

"With you still inside the grab?" snapped Murdoch. "Ye're blethering, laddie. Yon has a powerful grip – it'd chew ye up like a doggy treat. Come on out o' there, and we'll see if it's working."

"*F.I.D.O.*"

As soon as Yapper had wriggled his way out, Murdoch turned to Rascal. "Give it a try."

Rascal nodded. "Sure thing, dude – I'll move the grab..."

Murdoch nodded. "That's good. Now try closing it again."

"No problemo," said Rascal. "Snap it like a big ol' crab." He squeezed the trigger.

"No!" Sally turned from the window, her eyes wide in alarm. "Yapper's safety line is caught in the grab..."

After the first few moments of panic, Yapper felt strangely calm. It was really very soothing to be floating high above the earth in complete silence, with only the stars and the moon for company.

He felt rather sad that he wouldn't be able to save Foofoo, but somehow, what happened to either of them didn't seem so important now.

He spotted Sirius, the Dog Star, in the constellation of Canis Major. *In Greek myths,* he thought, *the gods made famous heroes and heroines into star clusters. Maybe that will happen to me and Foofoo. Perhaps we'll have a constellation called the Chihuahuas: it would be nice to go walkies with Foofoo among the stars, for ever...*

DOG STARSHIP CALLING YAPPER. COME IN, YAPPER.

"Sally?" said Yapper in a wondering tone. "Sally? Is that you?"

"*Of course it's me, you daft dog. We're still here, you know. We're trying to reach you with the manipulator arm, but you're just too far away. I don't want to fire up the engines to chase you because that would mean we'd change course, and we haven't time...*"

"Never mind me!" wailed Yapper. "Save Foofoo!"

"*We're trying to save you both! Can you see the ship?*"

Yapper craned his neck.

YES, BUT YOU'RE TOO FAR AWAY TO REACH ME.

"*I know*," said Sally. "*So what I want you to do, is throw your tool kit away in the opposite direction from the ship.*"

"Throw my tool kit away?"

"*Yes – Murdoch says, if you throw the tool kit away from the Dog Starship, that'll push you in our direction, and we can catch you.*"

"F.I.D.O." Yapper tried to work out the direction he should throw the tool kit. Then, thinking *here goes nothing*, he pushed with all his might.

The toolbox floated away. That seemed to be all that happened, but when Yapper turned his head again, he could see that he was nearer to the Dog Starship than he had been.

Spike's voice replaced Sally's on the radio. "*We've got you, Yapper. Rascal will bring you as close to the airlock as he can, and you'll have to push yourself across the last couple of metres. Come aboard – and hurry. We're running out of time!*"

Benji looked out of the flight deck window
and gave a gasp. "Why are all the stars spinning?"

"They're not," Murdoch told him. "*We* are.

Sally has to match the *Argus*'s spin, or the grabs will tear loose again."

Benji groaned. "The *Argus* was spinning and the stars were still, but now it's the other way round..."

"That's because we're spinning at the same rate as the *Argus*, so it looks to us as if it's not spinning, but it is, and so are we. See?"

"No," groaned Benji. "It's making me feel ill. Look at the earth. It's going round...and round... and round..."

"Good," said Sally. "Nearly there...nearly there... *NOW*, Rascal."

Rascal operated the grabs and...

"Firing thrusters to cancel the spin," reported Sally. "Main engine burn to change course – now!"

The engines roared and the Dog Starship vibrated as its powerful rockets strained.

Benji forgot about feeling ill. "Look! There's the *Earthview* – dead ahead!"

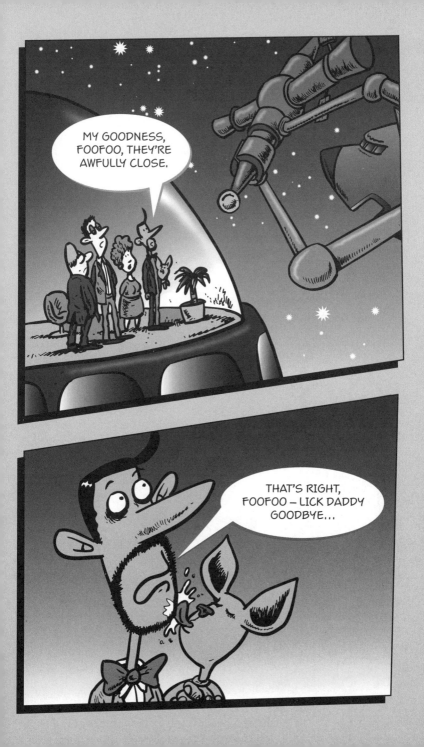

Sally wrestled the controls. "We're not turning fast enough!" she wailed.

"Murdoch," Spike snapped over his shoulder, "can you give us any more power to the engines?"

Murdoch shook his head. "I'm giving it all she's got, Spike!"

Benji closed his eyes.

Spike grinned at Sally. "Benji's idea worked a doggy treat."

Sally frowned. "Yes, but let's not celebrate too soon. This mission isn't over yet. We still have to work out how to get the crew off the *Argus*..."

"You're right." Murdoch was back at his computer, tapping numbers into the keypad. "And we won't have much time to do it, either. The *Argus* will re-enter earth's atmosphere in a few minutes. If the crew are still on it, they'll burn up like hot dogs on a barbecue!"

"Can't we just push the *Argus* away from the earth the same way we pushed it away from the hotel?" asked Yapper.

Murdoch shook his head. "It wouldn't work. We used up all our spare fuel doing that – if we used more trying to push the *Argus* farther out, we wouldn't have enough to get home ourselves."

"The crew are in the airlock already," said Spike. "Can't we just get them to open the outer door so we can pull them out?"

"Without spacesuits, they'd pass out pretty quickly," said Sally. "If we got them in here in under a minute, they might make it. Any more than that..."

A sudden thought struck Benji. "What about the Doggy Basket?"

"Man, the Doggy Basket is still in the experimental stage. I hav'nae finished testing the controls yet," snapped Murdoch. "For all I know, it might end up shooting all over the sky like a wee balloon."

"Maybe," said Spike. "But if it's the crew's only chance... I think I know what I did wrong when I tested it in the Action Station. If I can fly into the *Argus*'s airlock, we can get the crew aboard in no time." He clenched his paws. "All right, let's do it. Sally, get on the radio, tell the crew of the *Argus* what we're planning. I'll fly into the airlock and open the Doggy Basket's canopy to let them get in."

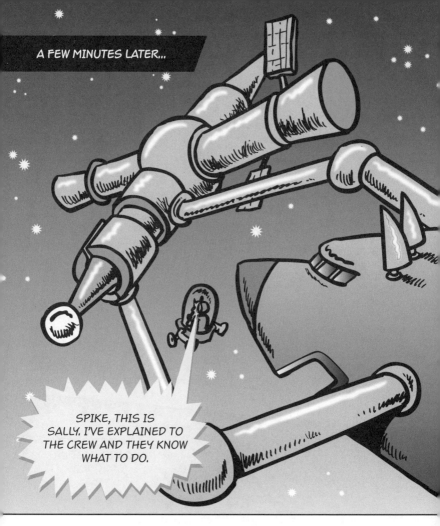

SPIKE, THIS IS SALLY. I'VE EXPLAINED TO THE CREW AND THEY KNOW WHAT TO DO.

"*There's just room for you to fly the Doggy Basket into the Argus's airlock,*" Sally continued. "*The crew will pump the air out and open the door to let you in: they can only hold their breath for a few seconds so you'll have to be quick.*"

As soon as the crew of the *Argus* were safely on board the Dog Starship, Rascal opened the grabs to let the crippled ship drift away and Sally started the engines. The Dog Starship pulled away from the earth – not a moment too soon.

One of the rescued
astronauts shook Spike
warmly by the paw. "Thank you,
Action Dogs, you saved our lives..." But
at that moment, there was a brilliant flash
of light from outside, and the Dog Starship
lurched violently.

"Good grief!" cried the man, "What was that?"
Murdoch checked his instruments. "Laser strike."

"Katmanchew!" snarled Spike. "I'd forgotten
about him. We must be back in range of his laser
cannon – we're under attack!"

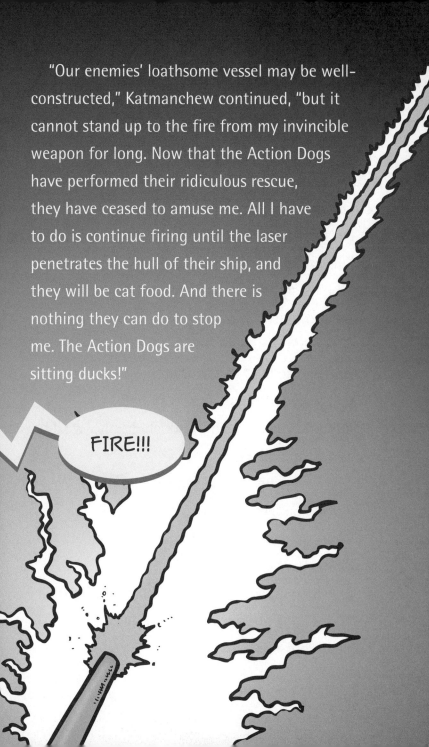

The Dog Starship bucked as another laser bolt struck home. The cabin was filled with smoke and wailing alarms.

"Evasive action," ordered Spike.

"I'm trying," Sally told him, "but Katmanchew must be using a really fast computer targeting system: no matter how quickly I change course, he keeps finding me again."

"Just do the best you can," said Spike. "We should be out of range in half an hour."

"In half an hour," said Murdoch grimly, "we'll be a smouldering wreck."

Spike threw up his paws in exasperation. "Well, can't you make this thing go any faster?"

"What do you want me to do?" retorted Murdoch. "Get out and push?"

"Boys!" snapped Sally. "Do you have to fight all the time? Look at yourselves!" Her voice tailed off. "Look at yourselves..."

MURDOCH! ARE THE LARGE COMMUNICATIONS DISHES DAMAGED?

The Scottish terrier looked puzzled. "No, they're working fine."

"And can you control them from your computer?"

"Certainly."

"And they're coated with a silver surface, like mirrors, aren't they?"

"Aye – to reflect the wee microwaves, ye ken."

"Then start pointing them towards that laser."

"Sally," said Spike, "do you have a plan?"

Sally gave him a savage grin. "You bet I do..."

"I've locked our communications dishes onto Katmanchew's laser cannon," reported Murdoch.

"Good." Sally let go of the Dog Starship's controls and clasped her paws behind her head.

Spike stared at her. "What about evasive action?"

"No need," Sally told him. "Now, we want Katmanchew to hit us!"

AND WHEN HE DOES, HE'LL GET A TASTE OF HIS OWN MEDICINE!

"O mighty Katmanchew," reported Katnip, "the Dog Starship has stopped trying to evade our fire."

"What do you mean, *our* fire, impudent wretch?" demanded his master. "The laser cannon is *my* weapon, and the accursed Action Dogs have undoubtedly given up all hope of escaping my wrath. I shall graciously put them out of their misery."

FIRE!

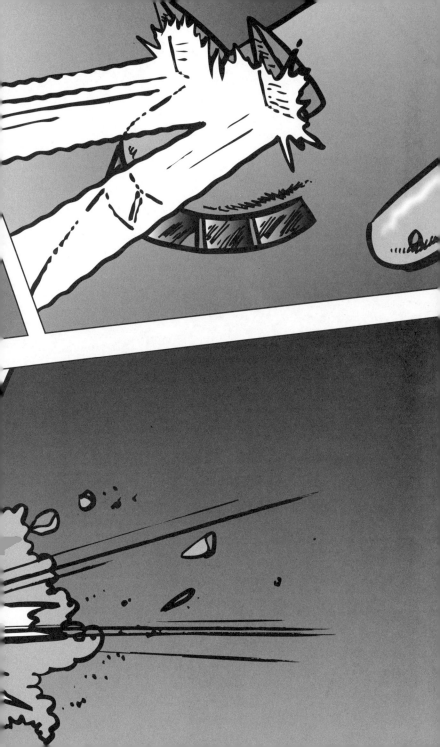

Katmanchew raved and tore his fur. "Prepare the *Katbird 1* for my departure!" Staring through the hole that had appeared in the cavern roof, he shook his paw at the heavens. "You'll pay for this, Action Dogs!"

Sally gave Spike a superior look. "Now who says that girls spend too much time messing about with mirrors?"

Spike grinned back at her. "All right, I take it back." Then he raised his voice. "Come on, team, back to work. We need to get back to base as soon as we can to pick up the Flying Frisbee. We're going to find Katmanchew. And when we do, I've got a bone to pick with him!"

As the Flying Frisbee soared above the island of Sumatra, the radio crackled.

"*Murdoch to Spike. Rascal, Yapper and I have delivered the crew of the* Argus *back to UN headquarters. They're all fine. Do you want us to bring the Bonecopter to look for Katmanchew? Over.*"

Spike flicked his *transmit* button. "Negative, Murdoch. The Frisbee is faster and more manoeuvrable than the Bonecopter. Return to base – we'll call if we need you. Over."

"*F.I.D.O.*"

WE'RE OVER THE JAVA SEA NOW. KEEP YOUR EYES PEELED.

Sally checked their position. "Our co-ordinates for the island match the ones the crew of the *Argus* gave us – and according to them, Katmanchew's island is dead ahead."

"There it is!" Benji pointed excitedly. A few kilometres away, a small tropical island with a volcano at its centre rose out of the sea. A thin column of smoke wafted up from the crater of the volcano.

"Do you want to land?" asked Sally.

"Yes...no!" Spike pointed. "Look over there!"

But as the Flying Frisbee chased the *Katbird 1* over the crater of the volcano...

The Flying Frisbee was flung upwards and shook violently. Thick smoke filled the cockpit.

Sally fought for control. "What happened?"

"The volcano!" gasped Benji between coughs. "it erupted!"

"No, it didn't," snapped Spike. "Would a volcano blow its top just as we were flying over it? That would be too much of a coincidence."

"Spike's right." Sally wiped her streaming eyes. "It must be Katmanchew's base that blew up. Maybe because of the damage we did..."

"Or maybe," said Spike darkly, "Katmanchew blew it up himself, to stop us discovering his secrets. It doesn't matter right now. Let's get after that felonious furball!"

Sally checked her instruments. "Spike, we can't! I'm sorry – our engines were damaged in the blast. We've barely enough power to keep us in the air – we certainly can't catch Katmanchew's plane."

Spike gave a heavy sigh. "All right. Let's get back to base." He glared after the *Katbird 1*, which was now no more than a dot on the horizon. "Katmanchew may have got away from us this time. But someday – there'll be a reckoning!"

OH, GOOD MORNING, SIR. YOU'RE LOOKING WELL.

NEVER BETTER!

"I've had a rest," boomed Officer Brick, "and some splendid nerve tonic my doctor gave me, and I'm a new man. I feel as fit as a fiddle! I could bite a tiger!"

"Jolly good, sir," said Janet.

"So, let's get on with that inspection, shall we?"

Janet's heart sank. "What – now, sir?"

"No time like the present!"

Janet groaned inwardly. All the Action Dogs were still out on their mission. When Brick called for them to parade in the yard, they wouldn't be there – apart from Master Yi and the dummy Yapper they brought out when the Chihuahua was busy at the Listening Post. Janet was sure that even Brick would be suspicious if all she could produce was one Peke and one not-very-convincing dummy.

"Well, come along, Kennelmaid Janet, no time to lose..." Brick hesitated as a dull roar sounded outside the building, which began to shake. "What's that?"

"What's what, sir?"

Brick went to the window and stared out. He gave a strangled cry.

THERE'S A GIANT BONE DROPPING OUT OF THE SKY! IT'S DISAPPEARING INTO THE GROUND!

WELL, I SUPPOSE IT WOULD, SIR. IN THE GROUND IS USUALLY WHERE YOU FIND BONES.

"And now there's a giant frisbee!"

"Of course there is, sir." Janet crossed to the window and closed the blind. "You know you've been overdoing it lately. Perhaps you've tried to come back to work too early."

"Yes, that's it." Welfare Officer Brick took out a spotty handkerchief and mopped his brow. "I need a longer rest...and more nerve tonic...LOTS of nerve tonic..."

"And a holiday?" suggested Janet.

"Yes, yes, good idea. A LONG holiday."

"You sit down for a few minutes, sir. I'll make you a nice cup of tea."

When Officer Brick had drunk his tea he tottered out into the yard, which was full of dogs happily running about.

Officer Brick glanced around. "Well, they all seem to be here. I think we should take my inspection as read, don't you?"

Janet said, "Yes, sir!"

Katmanchew ripped the photograph of his enemies out of the magazine and stared at it with hate-filled eyes. "You may have discovered my laser base, meddling hounds," he hissed, "but I have more unpleasant surprises in store for you. I shall rise again – and next time...!"

| BITE (attack factor) | ? |
| BARK (fear factor) | ? |
| SPEED | ? |
| RESCUE CAPABILITY | ? |

# ADD TO YOUR COLLECTION!

## SNIFF OUT **TWO** MORE EXTRA-SPECIAL GAME CARDS BY HEADING TO THE ACTION DOGS WEBSITE NOW!

# WWW.ACTIONDOGSONLINE.COM

Plus there's more info on your favourite canines and the world's most evil kitties, and unmissable downloads.

## For more fun reads check out
# WWW.FICTION.USBORNE.COM

First published in the UK in 2012 by Usborne Publishing Ltd., Usborne House, 83-85 Saffron Hill, London EC1N 8RT, England. www.usborne.com

A CIP catalogue record for this book is available from the British Library.

ISBN 9781409520344  JFMAMJ ASOND/12 02532/1

Printed in Dongguan, Guangdong, China.